Busy
Little
Fingers

By Judy Nayer

Illustrated by Christine Powers

Willowisp Press

Busy little fingers
Busy little hands
Clapping to the music
Playing in the band!

Busy little fingers
Busy little hands
Rolling out the cookie dough
Filling up the pans.

Busy little fingers
Busy little hands
Mixing cakes and mudpies
Playing in the sand.

Busy little fingers
Busy little hands
Painting at the table
Squiggles, lines, and hands.

Busy little fingers
Busy little hands
Pounding with the hammer
Banging pots and pans.

Busy little fingers
Busy little hands
Spreading peanut butter
Licking sticky jam.

Busy little fingers
Busy little hands
Clapping to the music
Playing in the band.

Published by Willowisp Press
801 94th Avenue North, St. Petersburg, Florida 33702

Printed in the United States of America.
A Creative Media Applications Production.

ISBN 0-87406-790-1

10 9 8 7 6 5 4 3 2 1